THE AMAZING ADVENTURES OF

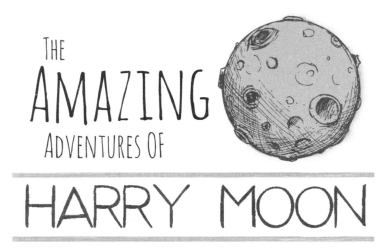

HARRY MOON

HAUNTED PIZZA

by

Mark Andrew Poe

Illustrations by Christina Weidman

rabbit publishers

Haunted Pizza (The Amazing Adventures of Harry Moon)
by Mark Andrew Poe
© Copyright 2016 by Mark Andrew Poe. All rights reserved.

Rabbit Publishers
1624 W. Northwest Highway
Arlington Heights, IL 60004

Illustrations by Christina Weidman
Interior Design by Lewis Design & Marketing
Creative Consultants: David Kirkpatrick, Thom Black and Paul Lewis

ISBN: 978-1-943785-38-4

10 9 8 7 6 5 4 3 2 1

1. Fiction - Action and Adventure 2. Children's Fiction
First Edition
Printed in U.S.A.

"I'm better than real. I'm true."

~ RABBIT

TABLE OF CONTENTS

PREFACE

Halloween visited the little town of Sleepy Hollow and never left.

Many moons ago, a sly and evil mayor found the powers of darkness helpful in building Sleepy Hollow into "Spooky Town," one of the country's most celebrated attractions. Now, years later, a young eighth grade magician, Harry Moon, is chosen by the powers of light to do battle against the mayor and his evil consorts.

Welcome to *The Amazing Adventures of Harry Moon*. Darkness may have found a home in Sleepy Hollow, but if young Harry has anything to say about it, darkness will not be staying.

SLEEPOVER PIZZA

To someone visiting Sleepy Hollow, the
town might feel a little spooky. After
all, one of the most well-known
things about the town is the statue of the
Headless Horseman in the town square.
The town also seemed to be frozen in time.
In a state of forever Halloween Night. Bats
were always circling overhead and the trees
were always stripped of their leaves, looking

like skeletal fingers. Most of the time, grey clouds drifted across the sky, threatening a thunderstorm that always felt just seconds away from starting.

But to those that lived in Sleepy Hollow, all of these things were just part of life. There was nothing *truly* spooky about it when you lived around it *every* day. The residents of Sleepy Hollow had lives just like people in other towns. They went to work and had family dinners. The kids went to school and played sports. The grown-ups paid bills and raised children.

One of those families, however, was raising a rather remarkable child—an eighth grader with the often-mocked name of Harry Moon. There were mysteries about Harry that not many people knew about. While most of the kids in school knew that Harry was gifted when it came to putting on magic shows, most of them didn't know just how magical Harry really was.

Still, despite his talents, Harry was really like any other eighth grade boy. He squabbled with his sister, Honey. He had misunderstandings with his parents, harbored a crush on an older girl (the lovely Sarah Sinclair, a junior at Sleepy Hollow High), and enjoyed spending time with his friends.

He was with his friends right now, in fact, sitting in Declan Dickinson's bedroom and playing video games. Harry, Declan, Hao, and Bailey were having a sleepover and as evening wound into night, they'd all decided to waste a few hours playing *Cosmo's Quest*, their current favorite video game.

Harry honestly didn't care too much for video games. He'd rather be working on magic tricks or reading. But video games were fun, too. Especially when playing them with his best friends.

They'd been playing their game for about an hour when Bailey put his controller down. "I'm hungry," he said, looking to Declan. "Is your mom going to make dinner?"

"You're always hungry," Declan said.

"Well, I'm sorry! My mom says it's a growth spurt."

"Then why are you still so short?" Hao asked.

They all laughed at this, especially Harry. He was actually the shortest of their group—an energetic and typically peaceful foursome that referred to themselves as the Good Mischief Team.

"Anyway, don't worry," Declan said. "It's Friday, and we always get pizza on Friday night."

"Awesome," Declan said. "I love pizza."

"Same here," Harry agreed.

Suddenly, Cosmo's Quest was the least of their concerns. When four eighth-grade boys get hungry at the same time, things can truly get out of hand.

Fortunately, the smell of pizza soon wafted up the stairs and into Declan's room. All four boys seemed to fall into a daze as they took in the delicious aroma. As if she had been summoned by their rumbling stomachs, Declan's mother appeared in the doorway holding three pizza boxes.

Declan's room erupted in applause, laughter, and cheering as the boys took the pizzas and laid them out on Declan's desk.

"Thanks a ton, Mrs. Dickinson," Harry said.

"Yeah, thanks," Bailey echoed.

"Hey, these aren't from Tiny's Pizza," Declan pointed out, giving the boxes an accusing stare.

"I know," said Mrs. Dickinson. "That new place opened earlier this week—The Sleepy Hollow Slice. I thought we'd try something different."

Declan shrugged as he opened up the three boxes. All three pizzas were decked out in tons of toppings. Harry stared at them for a moment, appreciating the steaming, meat-covered perfection. He wasn't sure if he'd ever seen anything so beautiful.

The boys grabbed slices right way. A chorus of mmm and yum filled the room as Mrs. Dickinson headed back downstairs.

"Thith ith gurb pitcha," Hao said.

"What?" Harry asked.

Hao finished chewing his mouthful of pizza and repeated what he'd said. "I said *this is good pizza.*"

"Yeah it is," Bailey agreed.

Declan also agreed with a nod but was too busy stuffing more into his mouth to say so.

From behind, Harry heard a familiar voice. He knew it was a voice that his friends could not hear...mainly because they could not see who was speaking. Only Harry could see Rabbit standing behind him, looking at the pizza with a frown. Both of his large ears were bent downward, following the frown on his fuzzy face.

"I don't understand how young boys can eat so much," Rabbit said. "Especially not pizza with this many toppings. Make sure you don't get any anchovies, Harry. Anchovies are...well, they're just gross."

"There are no anchovies, Rabbit."

"What?" Bailey asked.

"Nothing," Harry said.

"Were you talking to that imaginary rabbit again?" Declan asked.

Harry only shrugged and bit into his pizza. The shrug was enough of an answer for them. They knew that Harry was special and, as a result, he often did odd things—like talk to what they assumed was an imaginary rabbit. Their ability to understand such a quirk was what made Harry so certain that these guys were the best group of friends a thirteen year-old boy could have.

Harry was still on his first slice while Declan, Bailey, and Hao were picking up their third. Harry thought the pizza was okay...but certainly not as delicious as his friends were making it out to be. And not nearly as delicious as they had looked while still whole and in the boxes. Harry had eaten a single piece and found that he felt rather full. His stomach felt a little sluggish, like he had just eaten a mud pie.

While the others wolfed down more pizza from The Sleepy Hollow Slice, Harry picked up the game controller and played some *Cosmo's Quest*. He wasn't able to play for very long, though. His stomach started to really churn and he thought he might need to rush to the bathroom. He paused the game and lay down on the pullout bed Declan's dad had dragged into the room earlier in the evening.

"You okay, Harry?" Hao asked.

"I think so," Harry said. "I'm just feeling a

little...sick, I guess."

"Too bad for you," Bailey said, snatching up his fourth piece of pizza. "But more pizza for us!" Chunks of bacon, sausage and green peppers fell off of Bailey's new slice in goopy cheesy bits.

As the night wore on, Mrs. Dickinson eventually came back upstairs and told the boys it was time for bed. When the lights went out and the boys were left in the dark, whispering and snickering about the private jokes boys sometimes share, Harry did not join in.

Instead, he lay on his side and stared at the dark wall. His stomach was still aching and his head started to hurt, too.

"Harry?"

It was Rabbit's voice, very soft and concerned.

"What is it, Rabbit?" Harry whispered.

"Are you okay? Are you ill?"

"I'll be okay," Harry said. "I just don't think the pizza agreed with my stomach."

"Are you sure there were no anchovies?" Rabbit asked from somewhere in the darkness. "Anchovies could make anyone sick."

"I'm sure there were no anchovies," Harry responded.

"How about olives?" Rabbit asked. "Those are just as bad."

"No olives, either."

"Oh. Well then...I hope you feel better, Harry. Good night."

"Good night, Rabbit."

"Harry? One more thing..."

"What's that?"

"Seriously. Why do humans put anchovies on their pizza? "

Harry gave a thin smile in the dark and he was eventually able to fall asleep despite the pain in his stomach.

12

TEMPERS FLARE

When Harry Moon woke up the next morning, he was feeling much better. His stomach was back to normal and his head was not hurting. He was very hungry because he had not inhaled as much pizza as his friends had the night before. He was excited when Mrs. Dickinson called them down in the morning to a table filled with pancakes and eggs.

"Thanks for breakfast, Mrs. Dickinson," Harry said.

"My pleasure," she replied.

"Yeah, thanks, Mrs. Dickinson," Bailey said. "But you could have saved yourself the trouble and just got more pizza from The Sleepy Hollow Slice. That pizza is so good, I could eat it for breakfast, lunch, and dinner!"

"Don't be silly," Mrs. Dickinson said. "No one can eat that much pizza."

But this did not stop Declan, Bailey, and Hao from going on and on about how awesome the pizza had been last night. Even before they had left the breakfast table, they were making plans to get downtown to have some for lunch.

"Yeah, mom," Declan said. "Can we do that? Can we go down to The Sleepy Hollow Slice for lunch?"

"I don't know," Mrs. Dickinson said. "I really don't want your friends to tell their parents all

14

I fed them was pizza."

"Oh, come on," Declan said. "Please?"

"We'll see," she said.

"That's not a *no*, right?" Declan asked.

"Well, it's not a yes, either," Mrs. Dickinson pointed out.

Declan slapped his hand down on the table hard. The other three boys jumped and Mrs. Dickinson gave her son a disapproving look. "What was *that* for?" she asked.

"Nothing," Declan snapped.

Declan looked very unhappy with his mother. In fact, Harry thought he looked mad—which was odd, because Declan was not the type of kid that got mad very easily. Seeing his friend act like that made Harry a little uncomfortable. In fact, breakfast had become a little too tense for Harry. He did not like to see kids arguing with their parents, especially over something as stupid as pizza.

Still obviously upset, Declan stood up from the table. He frowned as he looked to his friends. "Come on guys," he said while still giving his mom a mean stare. "Let's go outside."

Bailey and Hao followed Declan's lead, but Harry waited a moment. He looked to Mrs. Dickinson and saw that she was very confused by her son's actions. Noticing that Harry was looking at her, she gave him a smile.

"It's okay, Harry," she said. "Go on out and play."

Harry obeyed and headed out with his friends. When he was outside in Declan's back yard, he realized how odd the events of last night had been. Harry rarely got sick. Even when he had accidentally eaten half of a slightly moldy apple pie last year, his stomach had been absolutely fine.

Maybe I'm coming down with something, Harry thought. But for now, he felt fine.

Saturday morning passed by in the lazy

way that weekends tend to play out and before Harry knew it, he was hungry again. Apparently, his friends felt the same way. When Declan's parents came out back to weed the flower beds, Declan approached them right away, doing his best to be the most cheerful and polite son that he could be.

"Hey, Mom. Hey, Dad."

"Well hey there, Declan," Mr. Dickinson said. "What can I do for you?"

Hao and Bailey gathered together around Declan. Harry lingered slightly behind, not really wanting to get in on pressuring Declan's folks. But he still wanted to hear.

"Well," Declan said. "It's almost lunchtime and we're getting hungry. We were wondering if we could go down to The Sleepy Hollow Slice."

Mrs. Dickinson let out a sigh. "We already discussed that this morning. Why don't we have a nice sandwich or soup here?"

"But *moooom*," Declan whined. "Please?"

Harry was astounded. He had never heard Declan complain like this. He sounded like a bratty five year-old.

"Declan, please calm down," Mrs. Dickinson said. "If you can just—,"

"NO! Just take us to the stupid pizza place!"

Declan's father gave him a look that made Harry's heart feel like someone had frozen it. He'd only ever seen that look on his own dad's face once before when he dropped a ladder through the convertible roof of his father's sports car. Harry vowed to never cause him to make it again. Suddenly, the Dickinsons' back yard was deathly quiet.

"Declan," Mr. Dickinson said. "Check your tone and don't you ever speak to your mother like that again."

"Whatever! Don't be so cheap! Get off your lazy butts and take us to the pizza place!"

Harry took a step back. The back yard now felt like an ice field as Declan was not only rude and defiant, but getting visibly angry. Harry, Bailey, and Hao looked to one another, surprised and a little scared. It was obvious that things had quickly taken a dramatic turn.

Mr. Dickinson stepped between Declan and Mrs. Dickinson. He looked at his son's three friends and did his best to look as if he was not bothered by Declan's outburst.

"Could you boys go inside, please?" he asked.

Harry, Bailey, and Hao all nodded. Harry was glad to have an excuse to get out of the awkward situation.

"Come on guys," Harry said. "Let's go upstairs."

They went up to Declan's room. Bailey looked out of the bedroom window, down onto the back yard.

"Wow," Bailey said. "It looks serious. I have never seen his folks so upset. It's weird."

"I know," Hao said. "If I ever spoke to my folks like that, I'd be grounded for fifty years!"

Harry looked out the window. "I can't even imagine what my parents would do," Harry said. He was pretty sure it would start with grounding along the lines of solitary confinement.

Harry had never seen a kid speak to their parents like that. Not even his sister, Honey. And she could get pretty snarky sometimes. It was sort of scary. Things were getting tense in the Dickinson house. Harry thought about calling home to see if his mom or dad could come pick him up a few hours early.

"He's coming!" Bailey said.

Harry turned on the television. As quickly as they could, the three boys picked up the game controllers and started smashing buttons like they had been battling the whole time. Seconds later, Declan came into the room.

Harry could hardly believe what he was seeing. Declan was smiling from ear to ear. "You guys ready?" he asked.

"For what?" Harry asked.

"Mom and Dad are going to take us to The Sleepy Hollow Slice!"

"What?" Hao asked. "After you spoke to your mom like that?"

"No way!" Harry said. "I'd be so grounded."

"Oh," Declan said. "Yeah...I don't know what I was thinking. I've never done that before. Dad got after me, really lectured me." He looked at his feet. "But he said he could go for some pizza, too. He had some last night and said it was really good. And mom said she doesn't feel like feeding all of you free-loaders."

"What?" Harry said. "Free-loaders?"

"Just kidding," Declan said. "My mom would never say anything like that. But we don't have much for lunch around here. So...The Sleepy Hollow Slice it is."

"Did you get in trouble?" Bailey asked quietly.

"Yeah," Declan answered, ashamed. "No video games for a week and no more friends over for a month after you guys leave," Declan said with a big frown.

"Yikes," Bailey said.

The four boys headed downstairs where Mr. and Mrs. Dickinson were waiting in the kitchen. While the mood was much lighter, Harry still felt very weird about what had happened in the back yard. But it wasn't very often that he got to spend a whole day with his friends, so he decided to tag along for lunch. The Dickinsons were nice and he enjoyed being around them—which made the scene in the back yard all the more confusing.

23

"I hope my stomach doesn't get upset again," Harry whispered to Hao.

Hao gave him a shoulder punch. "Probably just gas, Dude. No worries."

Harry climbed into the Dickinson's van with his friends. Even before they pulled out of the driveway, Declan, Bailey, and Hao were already talking excitedly about this pizza. Like it was the best in the world.

And now even Mr. Dickinson had joined in.

24

THE SLEEPY HOLLOW SLICE

The Sleepy Hollow Slice had just had its grand opening on Wednesday night after weeks of advertising in *Awake in Sleepy Hollow*, the local newspaper. Mrs. Middlemarch even gave them a front page story. Now, only three days later, there was a crowd of people waiting to get in. They were all talking with the same excitement as Harry's friends as they fell into the line at the front door. From where they stood, Harry could smell the pizzas cooking. Despite the way the pizza had made him feel last night, the smell made Harry's stomach grumble with hunger.

"Maybe it was just gas," he told Hao. "It smells great."

"Your gas?" Hao laughed.

This time Harry punched Hao. "Very funny. I mean the pizza."

After waiting for almost thirty minutes, they were seated. The restaurant was packed. Conversation and laughter filled the place. As Harry sat at their crowded table with Hao, Bailey, and the Dickinsons, a waitress came by to take their orders. Harry thought she looked tired and her hair was sweaty and messy.

"You guys are slammed, huh?" Hao asked.

"You can say that again," the waitress said. "It's been crazy! So, what'll it be?"

"Well," Mr. Dickinson said. "My wife ordered some amazing pizzas from here last night. What were they called, dear?"

"The Oink Special," Mrs. Dickinson said. "We'll have four of them please."

Harry felt his blood go cold at once. *The Oink Special?* Had he heard her right?

"Coming right up," the waitress said.

Harry watched her go. She made her way through the crowded pizzeria, towards the back of the building. She walked behind a counter where a cashier stood, ringing up someone's order. Behind the cashier, Harry could see part of the kitchen. Several cooks were bustling around back there, moving quickly. As Harry watched, he saw one man toss a ring of dough into the air that came back down in a perfect circular shape. This fascinated Harry; it was very much like a magic trick.

"Excuse me, Missus Dickinson," Harry said. "What did you say the pizza was called?"

"The Oink Special," she answered. "When I called the order in last night, that was the only special they were promoting."

"And it was *awesome*," Declan said. Bailey and Hao agreed wholeheartedly in a clamor of conversation.

"It was very good," Mr. Dickinson said.

Harry was still concerned about the name of the pizza. If the pizza was named after a certain servant of the town's questionable mayor, Maximus Kligore, then The Sleepy Hollow Slice was not the sort of place Harry wanted to eat. A shiver ran down his spine.

"I need to use the restroom," Harry said, excusing himself from the table.

He made his way through the restaurant, trying to find clues about the place. His past encounters with Mayor Kligore and his servant Oink had given him reason to assume that they were up to no good—even in regards to something as innocent as a pizza place.

Harry went to the front of the place and got a better look at the operations behind the counter. There were several cooks back there, busy putting toppings on pizzas and shoving the pies into a large oven. There was also one woman standing in the back, speaking on a cell phone. Harry couldn't be sure, but he thought he had seen her around Sleepy Hollow.

When she turned around and he could see her better, Harry knew her right away. Her name was Cherry Tomato, and she spent a lot of time with Mayor Kligore. She was also his chauffeur, driving Kligore around in his black, Phantom Lustro. Cherry caught Harry looking at her and gave him a devious smile.

Harry looked away quickly and hurried to the restrooms in the back of the restaurant. When he was there, he locked himself in a stall. He didn't actually need to go, he just needed somewhere quiet to collect his thoughts.

Rabbit appeared in front of him, out of thin air. Harry could pull Rabbit from his magic hat

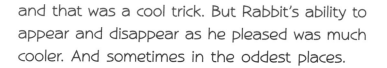

and that was a cool trick. But Rabbit's ability to appear and disappear as he pleased was much cooler. And sometimes in the oddest places.

"Something smells fishy here, doesn't it?" Rabbit said. "And I'm not referring to the restroom."

"Yes," Harry said. "But I'm not quite sure what just yet."

"Do you have your wand?" Rabbit asked.

"No. I left it at home. Why?"

Rabbit shrugged, making one of his ears droop over his face. "It's just a handy thing to have when Mayor Kilgore and Oink are around."

"That's for sure, Rabbit," Harry said. "But I had no idea about this."

Still...maybe he was jumping to conclusions. So what if Mayor Kligore somehow had a hand in the new pizza place in town? So what if one of the Mayor's best lady-friends was working here and one of the pizzas was named after

Oink, the mayor's most loyal servant?

Was that really any reason to start worrying?

"It probably is," Rabbit said, reading Harry's thoughts. "Keep your eyes open."

Harry nodded. "I better get back to the gang." Rabbit followed along closely behind him.

When he returned to the table, the pizzas had come out. Steam was coming off of them in waves and they smelled absolutely delicious. Harry sat down and took a slice. He watched as everyone at the table enjoyed their slices; even Mrs. Dickinson had a huge mouthful, scarfing it down with the same speed the boys had last night.

Harry took a nibble out of his and found that it seemed to taste better than it had last night. The cheese, sausage, bacon, onions, peppers and pepperoni seemed to call to him...and his stomach was happy to have the pizza coming.

But then he took a second bite. This one was much larger than the first and he took in a mouthful of meats and veggies. It tasted amazing but as he swallowed it down, his stomach started to feel weird again. At first, it wasn't quite as bad as it had been last night but it was quickly getting there.

Harry looked at the pizza slice with confusion and then set it down on his plate.

"You okay, Harry?" Mr. Dickinson asked through a mouthful of cheese and sauce.

"I'm good," Harry fibbed. "Just not very hungry I guess."

"I'll take that, then," Bailey said, reaching into Harry's plate and taking the rest of his slice of pizza. "Yoink!"

All around the restaurant, the residents of Sleepy Hollow were eating their pizza happily. More than that, they were *devouring* it, eating it in huge gulps as if their pizzas might fly away at any moment.

Meanwhile, Harry sat at his table, wondering why he wasn't enjoying it. If everyone else was eating the pizza like it was the best food on the planet, why was it making him sick?

The Oink Special, he thought.

Harry glanced back towards the kitchen area and a new feeling filled his stomach: worry.

⌒⌄⌒

33

While Harry Moon was having a conversation with a mostly-invisible Rabbit in the restroom, the kitchen area of The Sleepy Hollow Slice was as busy as ever. In the middle of the bustling cooks, stacks of toppings and the enormous oven, a rather clumsy creature walked almost unseen by everyone else.

This creature looked towards the back of the kitchen where Cherry Tomato was on her cellphone. She was no doubt talking to the man she referred to as Boss Man—also known as Mayor Maximus Kligore.

The small creature liked the Mayor quite a bit but he also *feared* the Mayor. And according to his friend Oink, that's the way it should be.

As the creature watched Cherry Tomato, she ended the call on her phone. She looked directly at him. She came over slowly and he wanted to back away but knew that she might have something important for him to do. After all, that's why he was here...to prove himself to Oink and, more importantly, Mayor Kligore.

34

"You're the one they call Ug, right?" she asked.

The creature nodded. Yes. Ug was its name, although he had no idea why. It's just what Mayor Kligore had called him.

Cherry Tomato sneered at him. "What are you, exactly?"

"A rat."

"Really?" she said. "Where are your whiskers? Where is your tail?"

"Hidden," he said. "You want to see?"

"No thank you," Cherry Tomato said, disgusted. "Look, I just got off the phone with Boss Man. He's going to need you to pull a double shift tonight. We need more delivery drivers."

"I'd be happy to," Ug said, meaning it.

"You haven't seen Oink, have you?" Cherry Tomato asked.

"Not since we opened," Ug said. "He's picking up more toppings, right?"

"Yes. But he should have been back by now." She seemed to think about this for a minute and then looked back down to him. It was clear to Ug that she did not like being around him.

"One more thing," she said. "There's a boy sitting over there with some of his friends. His name is Harry Moon. Do you know who I'm talking about?"

"Yes," Ug said. "Oink has told me all about that troublemaker."

"Good. If he happens to start acting strange, let me know right away. He's already come over here and peeked behind the counter. It makes me nervous."

"I'll keep an eye on him," Ug said. "Anything for the Mayor."

Cherry Tomato smiled at him and then left the

kitchen area. She headed into the large walk-in pantry in the back of the building where they kept the flour and toppings. It was more like a whole different room, really. Ug wasn't really sure what went on back there, but Cherry Tomato, Oink, and even the Mayor seemed to spend a lot of time back there.

Ug walked to the counter and looked out at the patrons. They were all eating happily, putting down slice after slice of pizza. All except one—that boy called Harry Moon.

Ug eyed Harry with great suspicion and did not take his eyes off of the boy until his party had made their exit from The Sleepy Hollow Slice.

38

CHEESE AND PARMESAN

For the first time in his thirteen years of life, Harry was glad that a visit to a friend's house had come to an end. When he arrived back home among his own family, he was relieved. Things at the Dickinson's had started to get weird. From Declan yelling at his mom to a sort of zombie-like trance among them all at The

Sleepy Hollow Slice, Harry had started to get very worried.

Back at home, his mother was feeding his little brother Harvest a meal of mashed up bananas. Harvest seemed more interested in painting his face with the stuff than eating it.

"How was your sleepover, dear?" Mary Moon asked.

"It was...okay," Harry answered.

"Are the Dickinsons doing well?"

"I guess."

He wanted to tell his mother about the peculiar way he'd felt while staying at Declan's house, but a small part of him still thought he was over-reacting. Something about the pizza simply didn't agree with him; that was all. Also, he didn't think it was polite to tell her all of the things going on at Declan's house. It was too much like gossip and both of his parents had always guided them to never spread news and rumors about other people.

But that pizza is called the Oink Special, he thought as he sat glumly in the kitchen. *And Cherry Tomato was in the kitchen at The Sleepy Hollow Slice. Mayor Kligore has to be involved somehow...*

Because of their history, Harry did not trust much of anything the Mayor had his fingers in. But to have some sort of evil influence over a pizzeria...well, that seemed a little far-fetched, even for Harry's magically-fueled mind.

41

"You look down in the dumps," Mom said. "Are you okay?"

"I think I might have eaten something at Declan's house that made me ill," Harry said.

"Are you feeling better now?" Mom asked.

"Yes, much better now."

"Good, because I'm making Leftover Casserole."

Harry's eyes widened as his stomach started instantly craving a dish the Moon family usually had on Saturday nights. Leftover Casserole sounded gross but there was something about the way his mom baked it that made it mouth-watering. She took leftovers from the week and stirred them all into one casserole. It was usually made of spaghetti and sauce, cut up hot dog or hamburger, meatloaf, and chopped veggies.

42

"Sounds great," Harry said, already starting to perk up.

Mary finished feeding Harvest his smooshed bananas and went to the fridge where she started gathering up the week's leftovers for the casserole. As she started mixing it all up, the front door opened and Harry could hear his father and young sister arguing about something. It wasn't too uncommon for Honey Moon to argue, but it was usually with Harry. For her to be bickering with either of their parents meant that something was definitely going on.

"But I don't see what the big deal is," Honey was saying as she and Dad entered the kitchen.

"It's not a big deal," Dad said. "But my answer is no, so that's the end of it!"

"Goodness," Mom said, whirling around to see what the commotion was all about. "What's the matter?"

"Dad is trying to starve me!" Honey said dramatically.

"I doubt that," Mary said.

"She was begging to grab a pizza for dinner," John said. "And it makes no sense to me because she just now wrapped up the church softball game. The coaches and the pastor chipped in and brought everyone pizza. She doesn't need pizza for two meals."

44

"Why not?" Honey asked.

"Oh, it's nothing to argue about anyway," Mary Moon said. "I'm just now putting together my Leftover Casserole."

Honey rolled her eyes. "Gross," she said.

There were three gasps of surprise in the kitchen from Harry, Mary, and John all at the same time. Even little Harvest mimicked them all and then chuckled. Leftover Casserole was usually the highlight of Saturday night in the Moon household. To call it "gross" was almost as bad as using one of the Really Bad Words that were sometimes on TV that Harry and Honey were never supposed to say.

"Honey Moon!" John said, clearly upset and disappointed. "Watch your tone!"

"But..." Honey said.

Harry gulped and started to feel very warm. He couldn't remember a time when he had seen Honey so mean and defiant. She was still holding her softball mitt as she stood by the kitchen counter but she threw it down to the floor in frustration. It made a slapping sound as she darted out of the kitchen and headed for the stairs.

45

"Dad," Harry said. "Do you know where the pizza from the softball game came from?"

"That new place that just opened," John Moon said. "The Sleepy Hollow Slice, I think it's called."

"Oh yeah," Mary said. "I heard about it.

You know, Marjorie Magpie said her kids just *love* it."

"It must be good," John said. "The kids at the softball game ate all of it. There were twenty girls and they tore through a dozen pizzas. It was all Honey could talk about on the way home."

"Well," Mary said, putting the casserole in the oven. "Maybe we'll give it a try next week."

Harry did not like the sound of that. But at the same time, he wasn't quite ready to tell his parents what he was thinking. With Honey already giving his parents grief, the last thing he wanted was for them to think he had gone nuts. Maybe he could get some answers on his own before dragging them into this.

Later in his room, Harry was laying on his bed, staring at the ceiling and trying to sort out his thoughts. Rabbit was sitting beside him, plucking at one of his long, droopy ears.

46

"What's on your mind?" Rabbit asked. He did that a lot. Whenever something was clearly bothering Harry, Rabbit was there to help him sort through it.

"Declan got mad when his parents told him no about pizza. And then Honey did the same thing this afternoon—and she *never* gets upset with Mom and Dad like that."

"I saw that," Rabbit said. "It was very uncomfortable."

"Mayor Kligore probably owns The Sleepy Hollow Slice," Harry said. "It only makes sense. Cherry Tomato was there and the pizza that made me feel sick is called The Oink Special."

"Maybe you should tell your parents," Rabbit said.

"Tell them what?" Harry asked. "Tell them that the Mayor owns the new pizza place and the pizza is making kids get upset with their parents?"

Rabbit frowned. "Well, when you put it like that, it *does* sound rather silly."

"Maybe if I can find out more about the place, then I could tell mom and dad about it. But even then, if I find that something bad is going on, what could mom and dad do?"

Rabbit shrugged. "One thing at a time, Harry."

48 Harry knew it was good advice. He also knew that they had church tomorrow and that it was something he could pray about. As a practicing magician, he knew that the Great Magician held the answers to just about anything. Maybe he would see a better way to handle this after church.

Harry fell asleep that night with pizza on the brain. He had a very bad dream about slices of pizza tearing through Sleepy Hollow. Instead of the Headless Horseman atop his steed in the town square, there was a slice of Veggie Lovers pizza. Pepperonis lined the street. Melted cheese slowly covered the roads in a delicious crawl of cheddar and parmesan.

And then there were the anchovies—the things that even Rabbit hated, and Rabbit didn't hate much of anything. They were in the fountain in the park, jumping up like tiny piranhas at anyone that passed and getting stuck in their hair.

Harry woke up drenched in sweat. He looked around his room, half-expecting a huge slice of pizza to be lurking by the end of his bed, dropping green peppers and sausage bits into his floor.

49

"Rabbit, are you there?"

"Yes, Harry," Rabbit said from the somewhere else in the darkness of his room. "I am always here. Are you okay?"

"Yes, I think so," Harry said softly. "I just had a dream about pizzas taking over Sleepy Hollow. There was pepperoni and cheese everywhere. Vegetables and anchovies and..."

"Anchovies?" Rabbit said.

"Yeah."

"That wasn't a dream," Rabbit said. "That was a *nightmare*."

50

School Lunch

Harry had prayed about his dilemma on Sunday and even nearly asked Reverend Allen for advice. But in the end, he'd kept it to himself (aside from the prayers to the Great Magician). Sunday went by without much drama. They even went to Staywells for brunch just like they always did. He was expecting Honey to get angry about pizza again but she remained quiet most of the day. She had even apologized to their parents about her behavior. For the most part, things were back to normal.

But on Monday, Harry was faced with the pizza dilemma again. Even before lunch, Harry knew that there was a major pizza problem in Sleepy Hollow. He heard about The Sleepy Hollow Slice a grand total of twenty-two times before the lunch bell rang. In the cafeteria, it was practically all he heard about. It had become such a popular topic of conversation that kids had started referring to The Sleepy Hollow Slice as just The Slice.

"My family has eaten there four times," Maggie Magpie, a seventh grader said as she stood in line waiting for her lunch.

"I had some Sunday," Clooney Mackay responded.

"We're going to have it four times at home this week," the quiet kid that rarely bothered to speak shouted on the way to homeroom.

Harry was saddened when he heard his own friends enter the conversation. He was not surprised when Declan, Hao, and Bailey also started talking about The Slice.

"We had some Friday *and* Saturday," Declan was telling Clooney Mackay. "It was awesome."

It was all anyone was talking about. Harry sat with Hao, Bailey, and Declan as always, but kept his head low and didn't take part in the conversations. For the most part, no one really even noticed that he was doing his very best to not take part.

It was not the first time that Harry Moon had felt like an outcast. Because of his magical talents, he knew he was different and was used to sometimes finding himself at odds with whatever was popular among other kids. Eventually, it had all blown over and things had gone back to normal without Harry having to change his opinions or behavior. But something about what was happening with the Sleepy Hollow Slice felt different.

For now, Harry was perfectly fine not being among the masses that seemed to be obsessed with the pizza.

That all ended when Titus Kligore came stomping over to their table. He carried an enormous lunchbox in his meaty left hand. As the Mayor's son, Titus usually had a lot of loser friends hanging out with him and today was no different. Today, Frankie Fowlson, the most feared bully in the school, was with him.

"What's the matter Moon Man?" Titus asked. He slapped his large lunchbox down on the table. It made a thunderous noise that made everyone at the table jump.

"Nothing's wrong," Harry said.

"You sure? You look like you're about to cry. Want me to show you my full moon? Would that cheer you up?"

Harry was used to the endless jokes made at the expense of his name. Titus was one of the worst, but Harry hot gotten so used to it that it barely even bothered him.

"Get a life, Titus," Harry said.

"Hey, I was just asking," Titus said. "I mean, you look bored. You not enjoying everyone talking about my dad's new pizza place?"

Harry was grateful that Bailey spoke up before he could stutter over some lame response. "You mean your dad owns The Slice?" Bailey asked, amazed.

"Of course he does," Titus said. "He owns anything worth knowing about in this stinky little town."

Murmurs of excitement filled the cafeteria at this news. Harry was relieved to find that Titus was no longer focusing on him. He was too taken by all of the attention. Harry lowered his head again, just wishing Titus would go away and that the ridiculous excitement over The Sleepy Hollow Slice would die down.

But it only got worse from there.

Titus unfastened the top on his lunchbox and reached inside. "It seems like you all really like the pizza from The Slice, huh?" Titus asked.

A series of shouted *Yeahs* and *Absolutelys* roared through the cafeteria.

"Well, to show all of you just how much my dad cares, he told me to bring this in my lunch today."

Harry couldn't help but lift his head and

watch. Titus reached into the large lunchbox and pulled out a pizza box. Harry's heart seemed to freeze when he realized that there was no way the pizza box should have fit inside the lunchbox. Harry figured it had been enchanted. He knew that Mayor Kligore knew Dark Magic. Harry wondered if he was seeing some of that dark magic at work through Titus's lunchbox.

Harry *really* couldn't believe his eyes when Titus pulled another box out. He set both boxes on the table and flipped the tops open.

For a moment, the cafeteria fell into silence. Harry thought the silence was somehow worse than their cheers from only seconds ago.

Harry peered into the two boxes and saw Oink Specials in both of them.

In an instant, the awed silence was broken as every kid in the cafeteria came rushing to the table. Harry watched as a stampede of hungry seventh and eighth graders came in a mad dash towards the two pizza boxes. Those cut off in line by other kids grew very angry and started to shove their way towards the pizzas.

Right before Harry's eyes, kids he knew fairly well started to get into fights. Several boys were rolling around on the floor, throwing punches. Two girls had their hands wrapped in each other's hair, pulling hard and yelling as they tried to get to the table first. Bailey had another kid, Fred McDooley, in a headlock.

He heard a few Really Bad Words as just about everyone in the cafeteria came rushing towards the pizza. There was chaos everywhere and Harry started to understand for the first time just how bad the situation was getting.

Three lunch monitors tried to stop the brawl. But they were getting pushed around right along with the kids. Even the teachers that were having lunch did their best to get in and stop it, but they were outnumbered. As Harry watched, he saw Mrs. Tucci, the Art teacher, try to break up a group of three boys from fighting. But the boys seemed to not even notice she was there.

And all the while, Titus Kligore grinned. He only broke the grin to put a slice of pizza into his mouth. Same with Frankie Fowlson. He was shoving pizza in so fast it was like a blur.

The kids that made it to the table first grabbed as much pizza as they could. They gobbled it down quickly while slapping away any hands that came out of the crowd of kids brave enough to reach for the pizza.

Finally Harry saw Mrs. Knapp, the middle school principal, come running into the cafeteria. She did her best to shout above the noise but Harry could barely hear her. When she realized that her voice was getting drowned out by the commotion, she placed two fingers to her lips and whistled. It was a very loud whistle, the sort of noise only teachers and principals could make. Harry had heard his grandmother make it one time, but it had nothing on the whistle that came from Mrs. Knapp's lips.

The ruckus over the pizza stopped at once.

All eyes in the cafeteria turned to Mrs. Knapp.

Even some of the teachers looked shocked.

"What in the devil is going on here?" Mrs. Knapp demanded. She looked mad—much madder than Harry had ever seen her before. It was sort of scary. She stood there with fists on her hips. Harry could practically see steam pouring out of her ears.

60

A few hushed apologies and murmurs of shame whispered through the cafeteria. When it was clear that no one was going to answer her, Mrs. Knapp stormed through the crowd of stunned students. She was headed directly for the table where Titus stood in front of the pizza boxes.

"Where did this come from?" she asked.

"From The Slice," Titus answered.

"The *what?*"

"The Sleepy Hollow Slice," Titus said. "Dad's new pizza place."

Mrs. Tucci came forward and eyed the scene. Her hair was frazzled and she looked terrified. "It was madness, Mrs. Knapp," she said. "Titus brought out this pizza and the kids went crazy!"

"But it's so good," Clooney Mackay said.

"Yeah," another kid in the back of the group agreed. "It's delicious!"

61

"I don't care how good it is," Mrs. Knapp said. "I have never in all of my years of education seen a scuffle like this! This is nonsense! I don't even know who to punish first."

Nearly every set of eyes in the cafeteria turned towards Titus Kligore. More often than not, he was the source of most trouble in Sleepy Hollow Middle School.

"What?" Titus pleaded. "I wasn't fighting! I just brought the pizza in!"

"Yes, well, perhaps you can help me figure out who to punish first," Mrs. Knapp said, beckoning him to her. "Come with me, Mr. Kligore."

A scowl settled on Titus's face as he slunk through the crowd and to Mrs. Knapp. She gently took him by the arm and led him out of the cafeteria. Frankie Fowlson disappeared into the crowd.

Slowly, the kids in the cafeteria started to act normal again. Declan, Bailey and Hao sat down with Harry, looking longingly at the pizza boxes. Still shocked at the whole turn of events, Harry also looked.

The boxes had been picked clean. Not a single crumb remained.

SECRET SAUCE

Harry, Bailey, and Declan were walking home from school. Because he had received a black eye in the brawl in the cafeteria, Hao was not with them. His mother had picked him up early from school.

"So what gives, Harry?" Bailey asked. "Don't you like pizza anymore?"

"I like pizza just fine," Harry said. "It's just that pizza from The Sleepy Hollow Slice seems to make me sick."

"That's weird," Declan said.

"I guess it is," Harry agreed.

"Didn't you eat half of a moldy apple pie one time?" Bailey asked.

64

"Yeah," Harry said. "By mistake."

"Seems to me that nothing much will make you sick if *that* didn't," Declan said.

"Well, look," Bailey said. "My mom already told me I could stop by there on my way home. She's working late and dad is out of town on business, so I'm getting pizza at The Slice. You guys want to come?"

Declan instantly leaped for joy and did an exaggerated fist bump. "Count me in!"

Harry got that queasy feeling in his

stomach again and nearly said *No thanks* but then thought better of it. As he tried to make sense of this, he also heard Rabbit's voice from behind him. "Maybe you should go with them," Rabbit suggested.

Harry looked over his shoulder and saw Rabbit hopping along behind him. Sometimes he could see Rabbit just fine but there were other times when he could not see Rabbit but knew that he was there all the same. Harry nodded to his invisible friend and Rabbit gave him a wink of support. "I got your back," Rabbit said.

65

Feeling like he was going behind enemy lines, Harry followed his friends down Witch Broom Lane and made their way to The Sleepy Hollow Slice. Harry thought the town had gotten even spookier. Or maybe he was noticing things more. Like Mrs. Crabapple had more rubber bats hanging from her trees and the Headless Horseman seemed just a little more animated than usual. It gave him a chill.

Declan was leading the way.

"Ahhh, pizza," Bailey said when he opened the pizzeria door. The delicious aromas slapped Harry in the face before he even stepped foot inside. His stomach grumbled at first but then seemed to remember how the pizza from The Slice had made it feel on the two occasions he had eaten it. Harry rubbed his stomach as a wave of nausea swept over him. He swallowed.

Because it was not yet time for the dinner rush, the three boys managed to find a table easily. Declan and Bailey were antsy; they could hardly sit still in their seats as they waited for a waitress to come by. It took only a few moments before their wish was granted. A waitress came to their table with a pen and a pad to take their order.

Right away, Harry saw that the woman standing by their table wasn't a waitress at all: it was Oink, Mayor Kligore's trusty evil sidekick. Only, as usual, Oink was dressed in a disguise. But Harry saw right through it, though. Oink's disguises were usually pretty bad and poorly thought out. For some reason, though—be it hunger or some sort of dark magic—Declan and Bailey could not see what lay beneath the waitress get-up.

"Can I take your order?" Oink asked, trying to make his voice as feminine as possible. Harry thought he sounded ridiculous but no one else noticed.

"An Oink Special please," Bailey said.

"Oh, that's a great choice," Oink said, as he jotted the order down on his pad.

67

"I know who you really are," Harry said, leaning close.

"Very well then," Oink said, ignoring Harry. "Your order will be up soon."

He seemed to be in a hurry now. Harry thought he had spooked Oink a little. It was clear that he was up to something...but what, exactly, Harry wasn't sure.

When Oink was gone, Harry turned to his friends. Could they really be so blind? Could they really be so stupid?

"Did neither of you see anything wrong with that waitress?" Harry asked.

Declan and Bailey shrugged. "She wasn't very talkative," Declan said. "Waitresses are usually chatty. Not that one, though."

"And she wasn't very pretty," Declan added.

You can say that again, Harry thought, still shaking off the sudden and very unsightly appearance of Oink. The thing that really made Harry uneasy about Oink, however, was that whenever Oink was around, Mayor Kligore usually wasn't too far behind.

"You okay, Harry?" Bailey asked.

"I'm fine," he said. "I think I'm just getting tired of pizza."

"Blasphemy!" Declan said.

Declan and Bailey had a laugh at this but

Harry didn't find it very funny. He did his best to seem normal as he sat with his friends, waiting for the pizza to arrive.

Oink slapped the latest order down for the cooks to work on and then slunk towards the back of the kitchen. There, he found Ug pressing out some dough among a few of the other workers. He hurried over to his helper and tried not to appear nervous. But the truth was, he was a little nervous.

"Ug," he said. "Take a break. I need you to keep an eye on one of our customers."

Ug stopped kneading the dough and clapped flour off his hands (which were actually paws) onto his apron. "Sure thing, Chief" Ug said. "You're talking about the Moon boy, ain't ya?"

"Yeah. He's here with his friends and he looks uneasy. I think he might know something and...*oh my goodness, Ug!*"

70

"What's wrong, Chief?" Ug asked.

"Your tail," Oink said. "It's sticking out again."

Ug looked over his shoulder and saw his pink tail hanging out again. Sometimes when he shapeshifted into a human, his tail seemed to have a mind of its own.

"Sorry," Ug said. He took a deep breath, seemed to concentrate very hard, and then the pink tail curled into a puff of smoke. "Now, you were saying?"

"Harry Moon could be a problem for us," Oink explained. "It wouldn't be the first time. Anyway, like I said, he looks a little uneasy. He's the only one in this place that isn't loving our pizza. He looks troubled."

"No problem, Chief" Ug said. "I'll keep an eye on him!"

"If he seems to be up to anything suspicious, let me know," Oink ordered. "This might be your big chance to get in really good with the Mayor. So keep them ratty, little eyes of yours peeled."

At this, Ug seemed to get very excited. He nodded and looked out into the restaurant. "I see him," he said. "Can't miss that inky, black hair."

"Good. You keep an eye on him. I have

business I need to attend to in the back."

"Yes sir," Ug said.

With that, Oink headed to the large walk-in pantry at the back of the kitchen. He opened the big metal door and marched inside. The lights were dim and the room smelled like flour, sausage, dust and—well, and something else that Oink couldn't quite name. He was pretty sure that to humans it would smell like some poor animal that had lost its life on the side of the road. Or maybe like mildew and some old rotting potatoes that got lost in the bottom of a pantry. But to Oink, it smelled delightful. He took a deep breath as he closed the door behind him.

"Boss Man?" Oink said. "You in here?"

"I am, Oink. Come on back, would you?"

Oink made his way through the dim room and reached the back of the room. There, in one of the farthest corners, Mayor Kligore and Cherry Tomato were prying open a big wooden crate. The top of it slowly popped open with an eerie creak.

"Sorry to bother you, Mayor," Oink said. "But I thought you might want to know Harry Moon is here again."

"Is he?" Mayor Kligore asked, delighted. "Good. Perhaps he won't be a problem as I originally thought. Is he enjoying the pizza? Is he having the Oink Special?"

"Well, that's just it. He looks very nervous. I think he's up to something."

"Well, that's not good," Mayor Kligore said.

"That brat was snooping around the other day," Cherry Tomato said. "He was trying to get a peek behind the counter."

"I've got Ug keeping an eye on him," Oink said.

"Good work," the Mayor said. "Even if Harry Moon *does* catch on, it will be far too late at this rate."

"But how would he even know what we're up to?" Oink asked.

"Because the boy has magic in him. It is a very different magic than what we know. His magic has light to it. It is a force of good and comes from a source that I have never been able to find. I don't think he knows how to fully use it yet but he may be skilled enough to figure things out that normal people can't."

Mayor Kligore looked into the wooden crate he had just opened and smiled. "But it does not matter," he said. "There is very little that even Harry Moon could do to stop us now."

⌒⌣⌒

When the pizza came out, Harry decided right away that he was not going to eat it.

This is what it must be like to be tempted, Harry thought as a chill passed through him.

Declan and Bailey were not worried about such things, though. They pigged out as they had before, grabbing up huge slices and cramming it into their mouths. Declan had a long string of melted cheese hanging from his bottom lip and didn't even seem to notice. Something about the scene made Harry a little frightened. It was like watching wild dogs eating a meal. He nearly expected his friends to start growling at any moment.

An idea occurred to him then and he was somehow sure it would get him the answers he needed. Doing his best to seem just as excited as Declan and Bailey, Harry grabbed a piece of the pizza. His stomach seemed to shrink when he touched the pizza even though he had no intention of eating it. Instead, he grabbed several napkins from the napkin holder on the table and wrapped up the slice. He had to add several layers to keep the grease from dripping through but he finally got it done.

"Taking some home to your sister?" Bailey asked.

"That's right," Harry said. "Do you mind?"

Bailey and Declan actually considered it for a moment. They looked at one another in the same way Harry had seen his parents look at each other when they want to discuss something but couldn't because he, Honey, or Harvest were in the room. It was a look filled with secrets and distrust. Still, their friendship won out in the end.

"Sure," Bailey said. "If I eat too much, I won't have room for mom's dessert and then she'll be *really* mad."

"Speaking of which," Harry said, "I should get going. I've got a ton of homework."

This was not entirely true, but he was eager to see if his idea would work out. He grabbed the slice of pizza and headed for the door with a wave back to his friends.

Harry Moon was so eager to leave The Sleepy Hollow Slice and get back home that he didn't notice the small, slouched over man staring at him from behind the counter...not even when a mysterious pink tail appeared out of nowhere and curled tightly along the floor.

MYSTERY INGREDIENT

At home, Harry tossed his book bag down on his bedroom floor and immediately went to his desk. He carefully unwrapped the slice of pizza he had taken from The Sleepy Hollow Slice. He frowned at the slice of pizza. He felt wobbly, his knees shook. He was actually *scared* of it. He was supposed to be this brave and

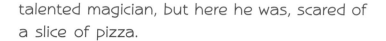

talented magician, but here he was, scared of a slice of pizza.

Beside him, Rabbit also seemed a little uneasy about the pizza on Harry's desk.

"What are you going to do?" Rabbit asked.

He had two ideas. One of those ideas involved his wand. He took it down from its place beside his top hat on the book shelf and pointed it at the slice of pizza. With the wand in his hand, Harry felt safer and not nearly as scared as he had moments ago.

He took a deep breath and said "ABRACADBRA!"

The pizza did nothing. It did not float or hover or explode. It just sat there on the paper towel, as menacing as ever.

Harry sighed and set the wand down. He looked to the slice of pizza and said, "I guess I'm going to have to do this the hard way."

"What's the hard way?" Rabbit asked.

Harry sat down at his desk and gently touched the pizza.

He had to admit, the gloopy cheese *did* look delicious.

The huge chunks of sausage and green peppers also looked tempting.

But there was something not right about this pizza.

Underneath its delicious appearance, Harry was pretty sure something bad was hiding.

"I'm going to take it apart," Harry said. "There has to be a topping on here that shouldn't be there."

"Be careful," Rabbit said. "If there are anchovies, you'll never get the smell off of your hands."

Harry couldn't tell if Rabbit truly despised

81

anchovies or if he was trying to be funny. Rabbit had always been there for advice and to lend a long and sometimes droopy ear, but he'd never been genuinely upset about something until now.

Using a pen from his desk drawer, Harry started picking the slice of pizza apart. He removed hunks of sausage, bits of bacon, and pieces of green pepper, onion, and pepperoni.

82

When he was left with nothing but the layer of cheese and the crust, Harry started to feel foolish. Had he *really* thought he'd find something sinister hiding in the toppings?

He was about to give up when he started picking away the cheese. It came off in thick gooey strands. Harry liked cheese and hated to see the cheese go to waste, but he placed it in the pile with the other toppings that were leaving a grease stain on his desk.

As he peeled the cheesy parts away, he saw the crust and the tomato sauce underneath. But he also saw something else.

Hidden in the bright red tomato sauce, Harry saw what looked like tiny bits of seaweed. He poked at it with his pen, picking up a piece and giving it a good hard look. He guessed it could be spinach, or maybe even basil. But no...this was a very dark leaf. Harry saw no shade of green to it at all. It was pure black, like some burned veggie that had been snuck into the pizza.

"What is it, Rabbit?" Harry asked.

"I don't like the look of it."

Harry smelled it and found that it had no

scent. He stuck out his tongue and licked it. It had a very faint taste that reminded Harry of burnt toast.

"Careful, Harry," Rabbit said.

Harry slowly placed the questionable topping into his mouth and chewed it. Almost instantly, his stomach responded. But it wasn't just his stomach; something else in him seemed to tremble. Harry wasn't sure where this sensation came from but he sensed that it had something to do with his magic. Whatever it was that allowed him to be a good magician and to see Rabbit while others couldn't did *not* like this topping.

Harry knew at once that this little leaf was what had been making him feel sick. He spit the topping out into his hand and looked at it.

"This is it, Rabbit," he said. "This is what made me so sick."

"Why just you, I wonder?" Rabbit asked.

It all came down to this one topping.

Harry took a piece of paper out of his desk drawer and folded it in half and then another half. He picked several more pieces of the weird-looking topping out of the tomato sauce and placed them carefully onto the paper. He then folded the paper over again and pushed it to the far edge of his desk.

"What now?" Rabbit asked.

Harry wiped his fingers on his pants. "Now we need to find out what that topping is," Harry said.

Rabbit nodded, staring at the paper as if he didn't trust it. Harry felt the same way. He looked to the mess he'd made while dismantling the pizza. His stomach rumbled with hunger. But this time is was a good rumble. For the first time in a few days Harry was truly hungry. He checked his watch. Dinner time.

As he walked downstairs to see what Mom

was making, he thought about the hidden topping, all black and leaf-like. Harry started to get a very bad feeling.

Were the cooks at The Sleepy Hollow Slice putting some sort of poison in the pizza? It seemed very evil to do such a thing, but if Mayor Kligore owned the place, Harry wouldn't be surprised.

I have to find out what this topping is, Harry thought.

Harry was quiet at dinner. All he could think about was the mysterious topping and what was happening to his friends. Harry chewed a chicken drumstick and gazed at the stenciled wall. The words his family lived by. Love. Peace. Kindness. He swallowed. Hard. Even Honey couldn't stop talking about the pizza. She kept spouting on how her friends, Becky and Claire were at The Slice nearly every day. Everyone loved the Oink Special.

He recalled the fight in the cafeteria over the pizza that Titus Kligore had brought in.

MYSTERY INGREDIENT

He wondered how much longer it would take before the entire town behaved that way. He understood that he may very well be the only person in town that could stop that from happening. He also knew that he had to act quickly before it was too late.

88

POWERING THE WAND

Harry knew it was risky, but he thought he might take a chance and go by The Sleepy Hollow Magic Shoppe before school. The owner, Samson Dupree was Harry's friend and mentor. A kind of magician himself, Samson taught Harry many tricks and often helped Harry talk through predicaments. Even if he was eccentric and wore a purple cape and a gold crown, Samson was the one person in town on whom Harry could rely.

In fact, Samson was the one responsible for giving Harry the gift of Rabbit. He suspected that Samson might just happen to be an archangel. Samson never denied it nor confirmed it.

Harry had not really been expecting the place to be open so early in the morning but when he looked through the glass door, he saw that a few lights were on. He saw Samson standing behind the counter, looking at a large book. Harry recognized the book even from outside. It was large and leather-bound and seemed to hold all the magic in the world. Samson called it a Grimoire or Book of Spells and had given Harry a smaller edition some time ago.

Harry tried the door and was surprised to find it unlocked even though business hours didn't start for another hour or so. He walked in slowly, the little bell above the door jingling to announce his presence. As always, simply walking into the shop made him feel at ease. The assortment of magical items warmed his heart. From magic hats to sneezing powder, Harry loved every inch of the place.

"Harry!" Samson said as he looked up from his book. "It's good to see you!"

"You, too," Harry said. "I didn't think you'd be here yet."

"I come in early from time to time," Samson said. "Besides, I had a feeling that I might get an early visitor this morning."

"Like a premonition?" Harry asked.

Samson only smiled and asked, "What can I do for you?"

Harry pulled out the folded piece of paper he'd used to hold the weird topping. He placed it on the counter and slowly unfolded it. Whatever the topping was, it had dried up since yesterday afternoon. It still looked dark but now that it was dry and the tomato sauce had also dried and flaked off of it, Harry thought it looked even more evil.

"Do you have any idea what this is?" Harry asked.

Samson leaned down and studied the topping closely. He pinched a piece of it between his fingers and held it up to the light. He turned it this way and that, making a series of hmmm sounds as he did so.

"I think so," Samson said. "But let me be sure."

With that, Samson bent over and retrieved a book from beneath the counter. It was another massive and dusty book that made a sound like thunder when Samson dropped it on the counter. Harry read the title along the spine: *The Potion-Master's Guide to Plants, Herbs, and Oddities.*

Harry's heart raced. He was instantly in love with the book. He could spend hours searching through it—or just about any other book in Samson's shop. While he was not at all skilled in potions of any kind, he had learned that the hard way when he tried to make himself taller using a potion. He watched as Samson flipped expertly through the pages, each flip of the page sent dust into the air. Samson would stop at a page, look back to the topping, and then go back to the book again. After three minutes or so, he stopped and pointed to a page. Harry noticed that Samson looked bothered by something as his eyes travelled back and forth from the topping to the book.

"I believe this is it," Samson said, tapping at one particular page.   Harry looked at the plant – black and green. Forbidding. "Where did you find it?" Samson asked.

93

"It's on pizza that comes from The Sleepy Hollow Slice."

Samson gave Harry the same sort of look Rabbit had given him last night— the stare was very direct and penetrating. Samson pushed back his Ben Franklin glasses and shook his head.

"This little ingredient right here is called hateweed. It is one of the most feared ingredients among potion masters and magicians. Not many people have actually ever seen hateweed. Even fewer have ever actually used it. It's believed to be a very hard-to-detect herb that comes straight from the Underworld."

Samson tapped the page. "See, read for yourself. The Underworld."

Harry didn't know what to say. Fear grabbed him in that moment and all he could think about was how much of this stuff his friends had eaten in the last few days without even knowing it.

"Samson, why does this hateweed make me sick but doesn't seem to bother anyone else?"

"I'd imagine it's because hateweed tends to make those that eat it very aggressive and mean," Samson explained. "I believe your body is somehow immune to those effects and the only way it knows to deal with it is to make you sick."

Harry looked at the strange leaf. His stomach churned just as the sight.

95

"This kind of evil," Samson continued, "is of a pure source and is in direct opposition to your magic. When you get ill, that is your body fighting it off. It's not too dissimilar from how your body's immune system fights off a cold or the flu."

"So what can I do?" Harry pushed his hand through his hair. "The whole town is going to be affected."

"I can't tell you what to do," Samson said.

"I can, however, remind you of the struggle that takes place on a daily basis in Sleepy Hollow. While it may seem like nothing more than a random ingredient on a pizza, this hateweed is further proof of the war taking place in Sleepy Hollow."

"You mean the evil things Mayor Kligore is always up to?" Harry asked.

"Yes, but that's only part of it. You've seen good magic, Harry; you are an expression of that good magic—a power called the Light. But you have also seen the Dark at work as well."

"Kligore," Harry said. "I know about his Dark Magic."

"Yes. And those that serve him," Samson confirmed.

"Like Cherry Tomato and Titus," Harry said.

"Tell me, Harry...have your family or friends eaten pizza from this place?" Samson asked.

"Yes. Lots of it. And they've been acting strange. My friends have been very mean to their parents and there was a brawl in the cafeteria yesterday because of it. Titus brought pizza for everyone."

Samson thought deeply about this for a moment. He closed up *The Potion-Master's Guide to Plants, Herbs, and Oddities* and returned it beneath the counter.

"I wonder, do you have your wand on you?"

"Yeah," Harry said. He retrieved it from his book bag and set it on the counter. "I usually don't take it to school, but with everything that's going on, I thought it might be a good idea."

"Absolutely," Samson said. He picked up the wand and studied it for a moment. He smiled and said, "Some very good magic has indeed come from this wand. But I wonder if it is equipped for a task such as the one you currently see before you."

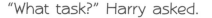

"What task?" Harry asked.

"Well, Harry...if the good people of Sleepy Hollow continue to eat food with hateweed in it, hatred will eventually rule them. They will live with hatred in their hearts...and the scene from the cafeteria you mentioned would be an everyday occurrence. Not just in your school, but on the streets as well."

"That would be terrible!" Harry said. "Halloween is bad enough. I always thought Kligore had even more evil up his dirty, rotten sleeves."

"It would be terrible," Samson agreed. "That's why you must tell your friends to stop eating there. And that's why I must make sure that your wand is capable of handling the fires and trials that are ahead."

Samson then clicked his fingers together. Harry's wand floated in the air and started to spin. Harry watched in awe as Samson twirled his fingers and the wand responded. It started to swirl and dance in the air as a white aura began to envelop it. Harry noticed that Samson had his eyes closed the whole time, as if in prayer.

With another click of his fingers, Samson opened his eyes. The wand stopped spinning and floated down, resting gently on the counter. Harry picked it up, his eyes still wide in wonder.

"I believe you're all set now," Samson said.

"Of course, please proceed with caution. And when you approach your friends and family with news of this new pizza place, remember to do so out of love and kindness."

"That might not be so easy," Harry said.

"Maybe not." Samson smiled. "But you have to try. Like I said...I believe this is a small step in the war the Mayor has waged on Sleepy Hollow. And I also believe that you can stop him."

Harry looked back down to the hateweed

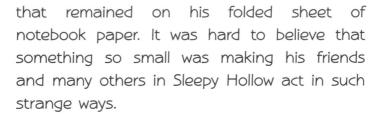

that remained on his folded sheet of notebook paper. It was hard to believe that something so small was making his friends and many others in Sleepy Hollow act in such strange ways.

"Don't look so upset," Samson said. "Remember, Harry...there is magic in you—the Light. You are capable of great things."

"Thanks," Harry said, finding it hard to take comfort in Samson's words.

He was going to have to go to school and confront his friends—to tell them they needed to stop eating pizza from The Sleepy Hollow Slice because there was an ingredient called hateweed in it that was turning them into angry lunatics.

It even sounded crazy to Harry.

He left The Sleepy Hollow Magic Shoppe with his head hanging low and a great burden on his shoulders. Sure, he knew that all kids had burdens of their own, usually based on their talents. But, as usual, Harry's talents had pre-sented him with the sort of burdens that only a boy of his abilities and understanding of the forces of magic could face.

102

WITH FRIENDS LIKE THESE

Harry pedaled his bike as hard as he could but he still got to school a few minutes late because of his stop by the The Sleepy Hollow Magic Shoppe. He managed to make it to homeroom before the bell rang but was unable to speak with Declan, Bailey, or Hao. He'd just have to wait until lunch. But as Harry walked down the hallways between classes he heard more and more whispered stories about families that had visited The Slice or had pizza delivered to their homes. And in each story he heard, one thing was certain: the Oink Special was a hit and they could not wait to get more.

The morning seemed to stretch on forever and Harry found it hard to concentrate in his classes. Finally, the lunch bell rang and Harry wasted no time in making his way to the cafeteria. He was one of the first students there, waiting at the table he usually sat at with his friends to make sure he could speak to them right away.

Students started filing in and Harry began to notice something alarming right away. Most of the kids were carrying brown paper lunch sacks or insulated lunch bags. Harry watched. Alarm filled his chest as he noticed that, those packed lunches all looked to feature a slice or two of leftover pizza. From the toppings alone, Harry could tell that the majority of leftover pizza in the cafeteria was from an Oink Special.

This is happening fast, Harry thought. *Word is getting out about how great the pizza is. It won't take long before everyone in town has had pizza from The Sleepy Hollow Slice.*

With this thought worrying him, he finally spotted Declan, Bailey, and Hao coming into the cafeteria. All three of them were carrying lunchboxes...which was weird because none of them ever packed. Not even when the school was serving meatloaf. Harry didn't have to guess very hard to imagine what was in their lunchboxes.

He was proven correct when they all sat down with him and instantly opened up their lunches.

"How's it going, Harry?" Declan asked.

"Not too bad," Harry said.

"You not eating today?" Hao asked.

"I'm buying later," he said. "But look, guys..."

All three of his friends pulled out their pizza at almost the same time. Declan and Bailey had theirs in large sandwich bags, while Hao had two slices of the Oink Special wrapped up in aluminum foil.

"What is it, Harry?" Bailey asked, bringing the pizza to his mouth.

"I found out something about the pizza at The Slice," he said. "I don't think you guys should keep eating it."

"Don't be dumb," Declan said, scooping up his slice. "Just because it made you sick doesn't mean we're all going to give it up."

"No, it's not because I got sick," Harry said. "There's an ingredient in it that makes you act different."

They all looked at him with odd glances. To Harry, it felt like he had just told most of a joke and they were waiting for him to finish it.

"Are you serious?" Hao asked.

"Yes," Harry said. "I found an ingredient in the pizza that makes people want the pizza really bad. Not only that, but it makes people angry and mean, too."

All three of his friends started laughing. Declan interrupted his laughter by gnawing down on his slice of pizza. Harry couldn't tell if they were laughing because they thought what he had said was a joke or if they knew he was being serious but found the idea crazy.

Either way, they just weren't getting it.

"I'm serious guys," Harry said, trying to sound important. He tried to bring a stern quality to his voice, the same way his father sometimes did when he meant business. "You have to stop eating it."

"Yeah guys," Hao said, joking. "We better not eat this haunted pizza!"

"Oooh," Declan said. "I bet it's possessed!"

"Or a zombie pizza," Bailey said.

Their mocking tones started to make Harry angry. Sure, he was concerned for them, but no one liked to be made fun of...especially not Harry Moon.

Before he knew what he was doing, Harry reached out and plucked Bailey's slice of pizza from his hand. Bailey stared at Harry. He seemed confused at first but then the confusion turned to anger.

"Give that back, Harry!"

"No, Bailey. You can't eat it."

"Harry," Hao said. "What are you doing, man? Give Bailey back his food."

"Yeah," Declan agreed. "Give it back to him. Don't be a creep."

They were all looking at him with anger in their eyes. Other than Titus Kligore and Frankie Fowlson, Harry had never had someone look at him with such hatred before. It made him feel very anxious and scared.

109

With a sigh, Harry handed Bailey his slice of pizza back. Bailey snatched it from Harry's hand and scowled at Harry.

"Not cool," Hao said.

"Jeez, Harry," Declan said. "What gives? It's just pizza, you weirdo."

Harry looked to the table. He was embarrassed and ashamed. But he also felt like his friends had turned their backs on him. They'd had their arguments in the past, but it had never been this bad. When he chanced a look up to them, Declan and Bailey were still glaring at him like they might punch him at any moment. Hao was too distracted by his pizza to care, munching on the crust of his first slice.

That was enough for Harry. Yes, he had to do something but he couldn't do it here. Not at school, and not with his friends. Maybe his parents would understand. Maybe he could talk to them and they could get to the bottom of this.

"See you, guys," Harry said quietly as he got up from the table. "I got to go."

"Good," Bailey said. "Go hide somewhere and talk to your imaginary rabbit about this haunted pizza that has you so scared!"

They all had a laugh at this, the sound filtered through mouthfuls of pizza.

Sulking, Harry left the cafeteria as Rabbit

joined him. "Don't let your buddies discourage you, Harry."

"This is serious, Rabbit. I'm kind of scared."

"I know, Harry. Remember I got your back."

"Even that can be hard to believe when it seems the whole world is against me. But I'm glad you're here and I'm glad you're real even if my friends called you imaginary."

"I am better than real. I am true."

111

As Harry made his way out of the crowded cafeteria, he heard delighted murmurs and the sounds of noisy eaters all around as they all greedily ate more and more pizza from the Sleepy Hollow Slice. He even caught Titus's eye. This time Harry looked away.

Harry headed to his Spanish class. But with each step he thought about the hateweed hiding in each of those slices and started to get very angry.

112

GLUTEN-FREE GIRLFRIEND

As a thirteen year old, Harry was used to feeling alone. He was also used to feeling sad for no reason at all. These were things that were all part of growing up according to his parents and Mr. Woods, the middle school guidance counselor.

He felt that way as he sat on a bench along the edge of the town square.

He was all alone on this.

"No," Rabbit said, sitting on the bench next to him. "You're never alone, Harry."

"I know," Harry said. "You've always been there for me, Rabbit. And by the way, it's a little creepy when you read my thoughts like that."
"Sorry."

Harry sat on the side farthest away from The Sleepy Hollow Slice, doing everything he could to distance himself from anything to do with pizza. As he munched his Headless Hoagie, Harry looked across the street to Haunted Hardware and Dracu-Latte. The hardware store was closed for the day but Dracu-Latte was still open. It was a popular hang-out spot for Sleepy Hollow high schoolers and every time Harry passed it, he wished he liked coffee. The smell was intoxicating but the two times he ever tried coffee, he'd not been impressed. He had no idea how adults drank so much of it.

He watched the high schoolers come and go as he took the last few bites of his sandwich. When the last bite was in his mouth, he nearly choked on it when he saw a certain girl come walking out of Dracu-Latte.

Sarah Sinclair strolled out of the coffee shop, speaking with a friend. Both of the girls were laughing and holding orange and black cups of coffee. This struck Harry as amazing. Something about seeing Sarah with a cup of coffee made her seem older somehow. It made her all the more fascinating to him and, if possible, he felt his crush on her grow stronger. He'd had a head-over-heels crush on her since she'd been his babysitter a few years ago. He had always feared that she saw him as nothing more than some kid she used to babysit even though they had shared an innocent kiss a while back following a magic show where he had wowed the crowd.

The girls went their separate ways and when they did, Sarah spotted Harry out of the corner of her eye. She gave him a wave and a smile and then, to Harry's delight, headed across the street in his direction. Harry's heart rate rose.

"Hey there, Harry," she said.

"Hey Sarah," Harry said. He swallowed the lump in his throat.

"What are you up to tonight?" Sarah sipped her coffee. Harry thought it smelled sweet. Almost as sweet as her.

"Not much," he said. "Just came out to get a sandwich from Deadman's."

"Yum! Aren't they the best?"

"For sure," Harry said.

He did his best to sound perfectly normal when speaking to Sarah even though it felt like there was a marching band in his heart. He also felt like his face was on fire and he knew he was blushing. Thankfully, it was almost totally dark out now. The streetlights weren't quite bright enough to reveal the red in his cheeks.

"And you're all by yourself?" she asked.

"Yeah. I didn't really like what we were having for dinner so mom let me get a Headless Hoagie."

"What were they having at home?" Sarah asked.

"Pizza."

"I thought all teenage boys liked pizza," Sarah said.

"I usually do," Harry said. "But...I don't know. Sarah, have you by any chance had pizza from The Sleepy Hollow Slice?"

Sarah frowned and rolled her eyes as she sipped from her coffee. "No. But good grief, it's all anyone is talking about. You know, there were five kids that got into a fight at lunch today. When the principal broke the fight up, he found out that they were fighting over a piece of the pizza one of the guys had brought it for lunch from that place. Isn't that crazy?"

"Not as crazy as you'd think," Harry said. "And you haven't had it yet?"

"No," Sarah said. "I'm doing a gluten-free diet.

"Gluten-free? What's that?" Harry asked.

"I'm not eating foods with gluten in them. So anything with bread is out. And that includes pizza. And anyone that tries making gluten free crust...well, it's never good. Yuck."

This might be my shot, Harry thought. *I might not be alone after all.*

"Oh," Harry said. "In that case...can I tell you something?"

"Sure," she said, sitting down next to him. "What's up?"

Harry tried not to seem too surprised, but having Sarah sit so close to him made him more nervous than he cared to admit.

"This is going to sound silly, but please hear me out," Harry said. "The fight you saw today over the pizza...there was one at the middle school yesterday. Titus Kligore brought two whole pizzas in and everyone went nuts for it."

"It must be some *really* good pizza," Sarah said.

"Maybe," Harry said. "I noticed people getting really mean after they've had it and can't have it right away again. It's happened with my friends, it's happened to my sister, and it's apparently happening in the schools, too."

"That's weird," Sarah said.

"It gets weirder."

Sarah smiled and said, "It usually *does* get weirder when you're involved, Harry Moon."

He was blushing so hard that he fully expected flames to come sprouting out of his face.

"Does this have to do with magic?" Sarah asked.

"It looks that way," Harry said. "But it's black magic...the kind that Mayor Kligore uses. And he owns The Sleepy Hollow Slice."

"Oh my," Sarah replied.

"Yeah," Harry said. "And I've tried telling my friend and my parents, but no one wants to hear it. They like the pizza too much. Hateweed sort of has a grip on them, I think."

"Hateweed?" Sarah said. "What's that?"

"It's the secret ingredient that's making everyone so . . . so angry and aggressive. That's what Samson told me. He looked it up in one of his books."

"Well, if Samson Dupree says that's what it is then that's what it is. You can trust him."

"I know. He never steers me wrong."

"So what can we do?" Sarah asked.

Harry couldn't help but smile. If he'd been a little older and just a little braver, he would have reached out and took Sarah's hand. "You mean...you believe me?" Harry asked.

"Of course I do," she said. "You're one of the most honest kids I know and I don't trust Mayor Kligore as far as I can throw him."

"I have to do something," Harry said.

"Any ideas?" Sarah asked.

"After I talked with Samson and he told me about the hateweed he powered up my wand. But you know him. He's very big on each of us figuring it out on our own. Free choice and all. So right now I have an awesomely forceful wand but I still need to find the hateweed. If I can discover where it is. I can put an end to it."

122

"Well, when you figure that out, I'm there to help you. You know my number, don't you?"

The wobbles returned to Harry's stomach. "Yeah," Harry said. He'd saved it into his cellphone a long time ago, copying it from the sheet of paper on the fridge that had her number in case of a babysitting emergency.

Sarah reached over and playfully tousled his hair. "I mean it," she said. "Let me know if I can help in any way."

"I will. Thanks, Sarah."

"Don't mention it."

With that, Sarah drank the rest of her Latte and tossed the cup in the trash receptacle. Harry watched as she headed down Main Street towards Paul Revere Avenue. With Sarah on his side, Harry was now more determined than ever to get to the bottom of things.

He peered over his shoulder, down towards the other end of the town square. Beyond the shadow of the Headless Horseman statue, he could see a growing crowd standing outside of The Sleepy Hollow Slice. It was hard to tell from where he sat, but Harry was pretty sure the crowd outside of the place was the line of people waiting for a table.

It was more people than he'd seen before. And now that he knew the pizza's influence had reached the high school and was even affecting adults, Harry knew that he had no time to waste.

He had to do something...and he had to do it tonight.

124

TOO MANY COOKS IN THE KITCHEN

Harry did not like being dishonest. He had told one serious lie to his parents the night he sneaked out to go the magic store on Ghenna Street in Boston. And boy did he catch it. That was the night he pushed the ladder through his Dad's car roof. But mostly, and definitely since then, he had been a loyal and respectful son and did everything he could to show his parents that he loved them through obeying their rules.

So on that Tuesday night, when Harry knew he had to sneak out of the house again, a pang of guilt gripped his heart. He hoped they'd understand when everything was over but still, he hated to break their rules. He was not supposed to be out on a school night after 8:00, so when he tiptoed down the stairs and out of the back door at 10:15, he felt like an outlaw—but not in a good way.

Fortunately he had managed to avoid Honey's prying eyes. She had a nasty habit of busting into his room without knocking and even spying on him. But she was busy with homework—Honey loved homework! Sheesh.

"Sorry, Mom and Dad," he whispered as he exited through the back door. He then turned to Rabbit, who was hopping along through the back yard with him. "Do you think they'll understand?"

"I don't know," Rabbit said. "But your

parents love you. If you have the best intentions at hand, they'll forgive you."

"I hope so," Harry said.

"Just don't destroy your father's prized possession this time."

"No way," Harry said. "Emma is tucked away in the garage."

They made their way down Nightingale Lane, dodging the soft glare of streetlamps. Harry carried his wand by his side and wore his DO NO EVIL tee shirt. It was far from a superhero costume, but it still made him feel a little safer.

Although the businesses of Sleepy Hollow were all closed for the day, the town still seemed alive under the cover of night. It was the kind of town where it was easy to imagine ghosts and ghouls hiding behind every tree, where every lurking shadow was not just swaying tree branches but some monster with eighteen arms that had an appetite for children.

And while Sleepy Hollow was the type of place where some of those sorts of things could exist, Harry was not worried about them. He had a worse monster to fear. With Rabbit at his side, his wand in his hand, and the favor of The Great Magician, Harry was able to make his way to the pizzeria without being frightened about the unseen.

It was quite a different story when The Sleepy Hollow Slice came into view, though. This was a physical thing, a building he could touch and see. And it was owned by a man that he knew was capable of very bad things.

Still, he had a job to do. He had to find a way to put a stop to whatever plans that Mayor had.

Harry approached the front door and peered inside. The lights were out but there was some sort of glow coming from the back towards the kitchen. He tried the door and was not surprised to find it locked. Using up all of his nerves, Harry drew his wand and pointed it at the keyhole in the door.

"Abracadabra," he whispered.

There was a soft click as the door unlocked. As quietly as he could, Harry opened the door and crept inside. He stayed crouched down low to the floor as he made his way to the counter. He could hear people moving around and, as he got closer to the kitchen area, he could also hear people speaking.

"You better have that truck ready to go soon," someone said. "Boss Man needs it before midnight."

"I know," another voice said. "I'm working on it. Almost done."

A third person spoke up. This voice belonged to a woman. Harry wasn't sure, but he thought it might be Cherry Tomato.

"Both of you cretins better get on the ball," she said. "Do you have any idea how important this job is?"

"Yes we do," one of the other voices said. "Ease up and let us do our job."

Harry suddenly recognized that voice, too. He'd heard the voice from a variety of disguises, but the face was always the same. It was Oink.

But the next voice he heard was even worse. It made Harry's blood go cold. He gripped his wand tightly as the voice of Mayor Kligore filled the place.

"Let's all calm down," he said. "After this next load of hateweed is harvested, we will be unstoppable. The Oink Special will spread all across the nation...and then perhaps the globe! So yes...what we are about to do is very important, but it's nothing to argue about. Stay calm, do as I tell you, and we'll all be filthy rich in no time thanks to hateweed."

"Yes sir," said the voice that Harry did not recognize.

The sound of shuffling footsteps followed this and the kitchen fell quiet for a moment.

"You got that last crate?" Oink asked someone, breaking the silence.

"You bet," said the unfamiliar voice.

"Great. Now let's get to the farm and get started."

Again, the sound of fast-marching feet filled the kitchen. When Harry could no longer hear footsteps or voices, he got to his feet. He looked behind the counter and found the kitchen empty.

He raced into the kitchen and saw scattered bits of dough and the now-familiar black fragments of hateweed everywhere. He looked to the enormous oven and it was like looking into a dark pit. It was what his dad had referred to as a brick-fire oven—an oven where food was slid in and heated by actual fire. The bricks that made up the walls of the oven grew enormously hot because brick holds heat.

132

The farm, Harry thought. Oink mentioned a farm. I bet they're taking the crates and the truck to Folly Farm to harvest the hateweed crop Mayor Kligore mentioned!

Harry knew he had to get to Folly Farm. He had no idea what he'd do when he got there, but he hoped he'd come up with something when the time was right. Besides...the best magicians, like Elvis Gold, Harry's absolute favorite, did their best work under pressure.

Hopefully that would be true for him, too.

Harry looked away from the kitchen and turned around, heading back for the front door and the dark streets outside.

He only made it two steps, though.

Oink stood in front of him with his hands on his hips. He smiled at the look of terror on Harry's face.

"Busted," Oink said.

134

THE FIERY FURNACE

Harry and Oink simply stared at one another for a moment. Harry tried to think of the best way out of this and came up with nothing. He was simply going to have to face Oink and hope he could be brave enough.

"And what are you doing here?" Oink asked.

Harry had no words at first. Then again,

he supposed he didn't need any. He raised his wand and pointed it at Oink. "Abracada—."

Before he could get the magic word out, something grabbed his wrist from behind.

Harry turned and saw something that looked sort of like a small man but mostly like a rat. The rat-part of the creature was using its long pink tail as a whip. It was wrapped around Harry's wrist, preventing him from waving it at Oink.

"Well done, Ug," Oink said.

"Thanks, Chief" Ug said, clearly excited.

"Thought you could stop us, did you?" Oink asked.

"Why are you doing this to the town?" Harry asked. He tried to pull his arm away from the rat's tail but he wasn't strong enough.

"Because we can," Oink said. "What better way for the people to understand just how badly they need their mayor than while constantly being angry at each other? When there are fights breaking out in the streets over something as simple as pizza, clearly the need for a Mayor's rule is needed. And hey... if we can make a few million dollars on pizza in the process, all the better."

"You can't...," Harry said.

"Yes we can," Oink said. "And we will."

Oink walked behind Harry, next to his associate, Ug. Harry watched Oink go to the large pizza oven, turning the dials. Something inside the oven kicked on and started to make a humming noise.

"And just to make sure you don't interfere with our plans," Oink said, "I think you need to take a trip into the oven."

"No!" Harry yelled.

"If it's good enough for the Oink Special, it's good enough for you," Oink said with a laugh. "Ug, if you please..."

Harry felt the rat's tail tighten around his wrist and before Harry knew it, his feet were sliding backwards. The rat was pulling him with its tail, dragging him directly towards the oven. He felt himself being lifted by the two minions and all of a sudden, that looming opening to the brick-fire oven was in front of him. It looked like the mouth of a monster, opening to swallow him.

Harry couldn't believe what was happening. He was being thrown into an oven that was growing warmer and warmer by the second. He could see the flames flickering inside. When he reached the oven, he grabbed on to the edge of it, trying to fight against Ug's strength. But then they gave one final shove and Harry was in the oven. It was so big that he could almost stand up inside of it.

"No, please!" Harry yelled again.

Oink and Ug responded by closing the door behind him.

Harry banged at the oven door as Oink tied something to the oven door's handle. He pounded at the door and found that it opened only an inch or so. It was being stopped from the outside by whatever Oink had tied it with.

With Harry banging at the door, Oink and Ug walked away towards the back room. Even from inside the closed oven, Harry could hear them laughing.

The oven hummed around him and grew hotter and hotter. The flames crackled and the racks and bricks beneath his feet were already hot to the touch. Harry was starting

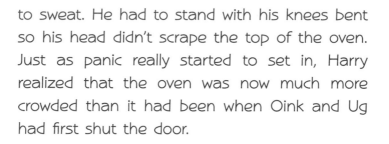

to sweat. He had to stand with his knees bent so his head didn't scrape the top of the oven. Just as panic really started to set in, Harry realized that the oven was now much more crowded than it had been when Oink and Ug had first shut the door.

Rabbit was scrunched up beside him. He was twitching his nose, causing his whiskers to twitch back and forth in a way that would have been funny under other circumstances.

140

"Harry, it's getting hot in here," Rabbit said.

"Help me, Rabbit! Please." He hated to sound scared but he was, after all, trapped in an oven. Within a minute or so, things would get too hot and then...well...

"Just calm down and concentrate, Harry," Rabbit said. "You still have your wand. Trust yourself. Trust the magic inside of you."

The oven rack beneath him was getting incredibly hot now. It hurt to put his hand on it. Sweat was trailing down his brow and into his eyes. Behind him, the flames were growing higher and hotter than ever. Harry felt like the back of his neck might go up in flames at any minute. Panic started to settle in. Harry wanted to scream or maybe even cry.

That's when he remembered visiting Samson in the magic shop. When Samson had enchanted his wand, he'd said something that Harry had found odd at the time, but now seemed very fitting.

141

"... I must make sure that your wand is capable of handling the fires and trials that are ahead."

Harry grinned when he realized that Samson had somehow foreseen this entire thing. As confident as ever, Harry raised the wand as high as he could, which wasn't very high at all, as the oven's roof was less than two inches over his head. He closed his eyes and did as Rabbit had suggested. He trusted the magic. Sometimes when he held the wand and sought out the source of his magic, words simply seemed to come to him. Sometimes it was almost as if someone had put the words in his head long ago and he was just now remembering them.

That's what happened in the oven – the words came and Harry spoke them aloud as he held his wand up.

I will not be burned,
I will not expire!
I summon a spell
to capture the fire!

142

A flash of light erupted from the tip of Harry's wand and filled the oven. Rather that shut the oven down right away, the spell seemed to bring the fire into Harry's wand; the flames from the back of the oven came rushing at Harry but they did not touch him. Harry was not burned or even singed as his wand sucked up all of the fire. The wand grew incredibly hot for a moment, so hot that Harry nearly dropped it. But the heat vanished just as soon as it touched his hand.

"Well done," Rabbit said.

It was then that Harry realized that the inside of the oven was no longer hot. He scrambled to the door and pushed hard against it. When there was still no give, he pointed his wand through the small crack in the door he was able to create.

"Abracadabra!" he said.

There was a snapping noise and then what appeared to be a large rubber band of some kind fell from the oven's door onto the floor. Harry pushed at the door again and it opened easily this time. He slid out and took a deep breath of the kitchen. He looked back into the oven, finding it hard to believe that he had even fit in there. For the first time in his life he felt big. He wiped sweat from his forehead and then exited the kitchen quickly.

Rabbit followed along behind like a shadow. "You know," Rabbit said. "It's about two miles from here to Folly Farm. I think we might need a ride."

"You're right," Harry said as he exited

The Sleepy Hollow Slice. It felt unbelievable to have fresh, cool air on his face after having escaped the oven.

He pulled his cellphone out of his pocket and pulled up a number he sometimes stared at, hoping he'd one day be brave enough to call it. He pressed CALL and listened to the phone ring in his ear three times before it was answered on the other end.

144

"Hello?" the sleepy voice of Sarah Sinclair said. "Who is this?"

"It's Harry Moon. I'm sorry to call so late."

"Is everything okay?"

"No, not at all," Harry said. "I know more about what Mayor Kligore is up to. And I was hoping you could give me a ride somewhere."

"Yeah, I can do that. Where are you?"

"I'm standing in front of The Sleepy Hollow Slice."

"Okay. I'll be there in five minutes."

∽∾

When Harry ended the call with Sarah, he sat down on the curb out front of the pizzeria. The clock on his phone said that it was 10:44. Hadn't Oink or Ug said something about midnight while he'd been eavesdropping?

Harry thought about his family. He wondered what his mother would do if she happened to wake up and checked in on him, only to find his bed empty. He wondered how long and harsh of a lecture he'd get from his dad if he found out what Harry was up to.

145

As Harry tried sorting through all of this, he was distracted by a pair of approaching headlights. As the lights grew closer, he recognized the shape behind them as Sarah Sinclair's truck. It was a beaten up old blue farm truck but with Sarah behind the wheel, it looked like a thing of mechanical beauty.

Sarah pulled the truck up alongside the

curb. Harry opened the passenger side door and climbed in. Seeing Sarah at such a late hour made him feel incredibly grown up despite the fear that surged through him.

"Hey, Harry," she said. "Hey, Rabbit."

Harry sometimes forgot that Sarah could see Rabbit. Samson had given Rabbit to Sarah. She delivered him as a present to Harry on the night of the Sleepy Hollow Middle School Talent Show. As far as Harry knew, she was the only other person that could *really* see Rabbit. Sarah and little Harvest.

Sarah pulled back out onto Main Street and pointed the truck in the direction of Magic Row. She drove fast, but not fast enough to attract the attention of Officer Ortiz who might be out on the prowl...not that he was often out and about after hours in Sleepy Hollow.

"Thanks for coming out," Harry said. "You're the best." Then he felt himself blush again and felt silly.

"Sure thing. Now tell me...what exactly is going on?"

Harry explained everything he had heard while in The Sleepy Hollow Slice. Sarah nodded, looking very alarmed as he related it all. It felt incredible to have someone not only listen to him, but to believe him when he talked about the hateweed and what it was doing to people.

She drove down Magic Row and turned left onto Folly Farm Road. Ahead of them, the night looked blacker than it had before. It was almost like the skies over Folly Farm were darker than anywhere else in town. Harry couldn't see a single star. Slowly, the shapes of the farm's buildings came into view. They stood out just a bit darker than the night around them: the barns, the sheds and the large house that the Mayor lived in.

Harry's heart felt like it was trying to shrivel up inside his chest as the farm got closer. He gripped his wand tight as Sarah slowed the truck to a crawl as they neared the farm's entrance. She parked it on the side of the road and cut off the headlights.

"Okay," Sarah said. "Let's go."

"I think you should stay here," Harry said. "Please...stay here. Stay safe."

"Don't you need some help?" she asked.

"I have Rabbit and my magic," Harry said. "I'll be fine." He wasn't sure if this was true or not, but it felt good to say it

"Okay," she said. "But if you get into any sort of trouble, you better call me."

"I will. I promise."

He reached for the door handle but before he could grab it, Sarah leaned over and kissed him on the cheek.

"Be careful," she said.

"I will," Harry replied, the kiss sent a jolt of

energy and confidence into him.

He got out of the truck and waited for Rabbit to hop down next to him. Side by side, they walked away from Sarah Sinclair's truck and started down the long driveway that led to Folly Farms.

150

AT FOLLY FARM

As he walked towards the barn in the darkness ahead, the gravel of the driveway crunched under Harry's shoes. It was a spooky sound that had him jumping at every single shadow they passed. But even though the sounds of the gravel sounded impossibly loud, it did not keep Harry from hearing the slight noises coming from further ahead.

There were muffled voices and the sound of things being moved. Harry was certain Kligore's hounds were fast at doing their boss's nefarious and evil bidding.

He passed the Mayor's house and continued down the driveway. As they came to a hill in the driveway, he saw where the noises were coming from. Way down the hill, two trucks were parked in front of a big barn. There were a few people walking back and forth from the trucks to the barn.

Harry looked to his right and saw a field that was filled with hay bales. Maybe if he could hide behind those, he could make it to the bottom of the hill to see what was going on. He darted into the field and used the bales of hay to make his way down the hill unseen.

As he made his way closer to the barn, Harry got a better view of what was taking place. He could clearly see Mayor Kligore standing at the back of a truck. Down the side of the truck, in white, stenciled letters, were the words: WE DRIVE BY NIGHT.

The Mayor was speaking to two other figures that were going back and forth into the barn. As Harry watched, one of these figures opened a huge door along the back of the barn. When light spilled out of the doorway, Harry could see what sat behind the barn and its shadow.

That's when the night seemed to get even worse. Even darker. A crackle of lightning and boom of thunder sounded in the distance.

Behind the barn, the field of hay bales came to an end and another field began. It was hard to tell what was growing in that field because it was so dark, but Harry was pretty sure it was some sort of vine. He looked back to the barn and saw the two other figures huddled at the large back door. Harry ran to the next hay bale and could then see these two figures as well. He wasn't at all surprised to find that it was Oink and Ug.

For the first time, Harry thought it might have been a bad idea to come here all by himself. While he'd managed to get the best

of Mayor Kligore in the past, the task set before him now seemed almost impossible.

"What do I do, Rabbit?" Harry asked.

Rabbit, hunkered down behind the hay bale. He gave Harry one of the most sincere looks the two had ever shared. Harry saw something in Rabbit's eyes that went further than simple knowledge. There was something else there...something Harry didn't think he'd ever fully understand.

"Do what's right," Rabbit said. "Trust in your magic, Harry. Be strong and courageous and you won't go wrong."

Harry nodded and, with his wand held tightly by his side, he stepped out from behind the hay bale and went running down towards the barn. He made it to the side of the barn without being seen and crept along the side to the large back door. For the second time that night, Harry listened in on the evil plans of Oink and Ug.

"How much longer?" Ug asked.

"Twenty more minutes," Oink said. "We can't pick a single vine until midnight. A minute before or a minute after and the hate-weed will lose its power."

Harry looked back out to the vines that were lying low to the ground. They stretched out as far as Harry could see in the dark.

All of that is hateweed, Harry thought. *There's enough here to go on a million pizzas!*

Harry tried to summon his courage and step out to confront Kligore's Hell Hounds—Oink and Ug. He thought of Sarah sitting in her truck, waiting for him. How great would it be if he could save the day and have her right there to celebrate with?

Of course, saving the town was more important. He had to act fast. He had to—

"Well, hello Harry Moon!"

The voice came from behind him and scared Harry so badly that he nearly dropped his wand. He wheeled around and saw Mayor Kligore standing there. He'd snuck up behind Harry and now they were standing face-to-face. While the Mayor had indeed scared Harry in that moment, Harry was also filled with defiance and anger. He knew that anger could be a bad thing, but he also knew that there was a thing called *righteous anger.* He was pretty sure that's what he felt towards the Mayor.

"You can't do this," Harry spat.

"You silly child," the Mayor said. "I suppose you're going to try to stop me?"

"You bet I am."

"Oink," Mayor Kligore yelled. "Would you come here, please?"

Oink hurried over along the side of the barn. His eyes went wide when he saw Harry. "But I tossed you in the oven!" Oink exclaimed. "How...when...what...?"

"You left him alone," Mayor Kligore said. "I've told you time and time again, Oink...Harry Moon has power. He has the *real magic.*"

Oink gave a low growl in his throat and

regarded Harry with a menacing look. "It won't happen again, Boss Man," Oink said. "You have my word on that."

"No, it won't" the Mayor said. "Because I have Mr. Moon in my possession now. And I'm even going to have him help us pick our hateweed crop."

"I'm not going to help you," Harry said.

"Oh, but you will," Mayor Kligore said with a sly smile. "Think of it, Harry...the Oink Special could be served in schools. It could be sold as frozen pizza all over the nation. It could even go global!

"But why?" Harry asked. "Why would you want to make everyone mean to one another?"

"People's anger makes them easy to control," Mayor Kligore said. "And since Folly Farm is the only place in the world that is capable of growing hateweed, the demand for my pizza will be through the roof. I'll be rich! And you, Harry...well, if you help us pick this crop, we can forget all of our differences. Your magic is powerful, Harry. I know that, and I respect it. We can be partners, Harry. Your magic and my magic together can rule everything." Then Kligore let go a wicked laugh.

"No way," Harry said.

"Very well, then," Mayor Kligore said. "Then I have no choice but to make you help us with this crop."

159

Mayor Kligore lifted his wand. He pulled it out so quickly that Harry didn't even see where he had drawn it from. With his wand out, a dark, knotty piece of wood, he opened his mouth to speak an incantation towards Harry. But Harry had much more practice with his wand thanks to countless magic shows and much practice. He drew his wand up and shouted *"ABRACADABRA!"* at the top of his lungs before Mayor Kligore could make a sound.

Mayor Kligore's wand went flying from his hand. At the same moment, a blast of white light came out of Harry's wand and enveloped the Mayor. Mayor Kligore slapped at the light, trying to get it to go away but it clung to him. He shrieked out in fear and tried to run away but the light would not let him move.

Harry heard movement behind him. He turned around and saw Oink and Ug running towards him. Ug was in the lead, his pink tail darting up into the air like a whip. When it came down, Harry dodged it just in time. Harry then ran to the right and the tail followed, just as he had hoped.

Oink tripped over Ug's long pink tail and the two went sprawling to the ground. Had the night not been so dark and there wasn't an enormous crop of hateweed in front of him, Harry thought the sight of the two tripping over one another would have been funny.

Harry aimed his wand at the bumbling villains and again shouted *"ABRACADABRA!"*

The same white light that had trapped Mayor Kligore came out of his wand and fell on Oink and Ug. It trapped them like a net and neither of them were able to get up from the ground. Oink made a series of growling noises and Ug started squeaking—they were very loud squeaks, reminding Harry that underneath Ug's scary appearance, he was really nothing more than a rat.

"Now what?" Mayor Kligore said from under his trap of white light. "You think you've won, Harry Moon? I suggest you run!"

Harry believed it, and the thought of running back to Sarah's truck was tempting. But he remembered what Rabbit had told him. He had used words that he'd heard in church on Sunday mornings—words that seemed so simple but meant so much.

Be strong and courageous.

Harry looked back out to the field of hateweed. He had seen what just a few bits of the dark vegetable could do to someone. Trying to imagine what an entire field of the stuff could do was frightening.

Harry wasn't quite sure what he needed to do, but he trusted that the real magic would lead him. He stepped towards the vines of hateweed and looked out over the field. It may have just been a trick played by the shadows and darkness of the night, but it looked like the vines were moving, slithering slowly like snakes.

As he stood there, Harry felt something warm in his right hand. He looked to his hand and saw only his wand. It seemed to be getting warm...not just warm, but almost hot to the touch.

The oven, Harry thought.

He recalled how the spell he'd cast in the oven had zapped the heat away and how, for a moment, his wand had gotten very hot. An idea occurred to him then and when it did, he knew he had the answer.

He stood firmly as he held his wand out towards the hateweed. When he did, he saw Rabbit next to him. But he also felt something else, almost like someone else was there with them, watching it all happen. Harry gave a small smile, wondering if this was the Great Magician joining him, making sure he succeeded.

Harry took a deep breath as the wand grew hotter under his fingers. He then recited the words that seemed to come to him from the night itself.

Fire inside, burning and freed
scorch the earth and burn this weed!

163

Fire came bursting forth from Harry's wand so quickly that he thought it might burn his fingers. It shook the wand, but Harry held tightly as the flames kept coming out. The flames lit up the night and Harry could see the vines clearly. They *had* been moving and now, as the flames touched the vines, they started to shrivel up.

Behind him, Mayor Kligore let out a scream of defeat. "No! All of my hard work! Harry Moon, I will not forget this, you meddling magician!"

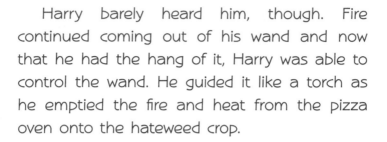

Harry barely heard him, though. Fire continued coming out of his wand and now that he had the hang of it, Harry was able to control the wand. He guided it like a torch as he emptied the fire and heat from the pizza oven onto the hateweed crop.

He bathed the ground in fire. He could hear the crackling noises of the hateweed and it was like music to his ears. It was weird but it sort of sounded like a thousand arguing voices.

After a few more seconds, the wand had no fire left to give. But that was fine. From what Harry could tell, the entire hateweed crop was in flames.

He gave one final look back to Mayor Kligore, Oink, and Ug before running back up the hill beside the hay bales. When he arrived at the gravel driveway, he looked back and saw the fire dancing along the hateweed vines. The flames were growing larger and Harry wondered if they may get out of hand and spread elsewhere into Sleepy Hollow.

For the last time of the night, Harry drew his wand and pointed it in the direction of the fire. By now, the crops would be destroyed, and that was the important thing. He'd done his job and now he needed to make sure he didn't accidentally set the whole town on fire.

He waved his wand and recited: *"Rain, rain, come and stay!"*

A small grey cloud formed over the hateweed crop and started to sprinkle rain down on the fire. Harry stood there until he saw the flames shrinking down and then headed farther back down the driveway.

Sarah's truck was still parked there and when he opened the door, he couldn't believe how glad he was to see her.

"I saw something glowing," Sarah said, worried. "Was it fire?"

"Yeah," Harry said. "But it'll be out soon."

"Did you stop the Mayor?"

"Yes, I did," Harry said, realizing that he was very tired.

"What did you do?" Sarah asked.

Harry smiled and looked to Rabbit as he climbed into the truck beside him.

"Nothing, really," Harry said. "I was just strong and courageous."

JUST DESSERTS

Two nights later, Harry was sitting at his desk. He was studying for a test that was coming up in World History but he was having a hard time focusing. He kept seeing flames dancing atop Folly Farm. He still couldn't believe he'd done it.

More than that, he couldn't believe he still hadn't told his parents.

It made him feel guilty. And he knew that telling them the truth was the right thing to do. But...man, they were going to be so mad.

As he studied, there was a knock at his door. It opened up and his Mom poked her head in. "Any ideas for dinner?" she asked.

Harry smiled. "Pizza?" he asked.

"Really? After everything that's happened, you want pizza?"

Harry shrugged. The day after he had destroyed the hateweed crop, The Sleepy Hollow Slice had closed down unexpectedly. Since then, Tiny's Pizza had seen a surge in business. And, quite honestly, Harry had been craving pizza very badly ever since the nasty business with The Sleepy Hollow Slice. Seeing pizza in front of him that he knew he could not eat had been torture. After all of that, he could go for a good pepperoni pizza right about now.

"Well," Mom said, "I'll check with everyone else and see if that's what they want."

"Cool," Harry said.

Mary started closing the door and when she did, Harry spoke up.

"Hey mom," he said.

"Yes, dear?"

"There's something I need to tell you."

It was all on the tip of his tongue but it was so hard to get it out. He didn't want to disappoint his parents. But he also didn't want to get in trouble.

He looked to his bed, where Rabbit was sitting with a tattered copy of his favorite book, *Beyond Quantum Physics*. He returned Harry's gaze and nodded his encouragement.

Be strong and courageous, Harry thought.

And with that, he told his mother everything. She was shocked and genuinely alarmed throughout the story, but in the end it came down to one single thing. It was the same thing Mom used to end most tense conversations with her children.

She stepped forward and gave Harry a hug.

"So, you're okay with it all?" Harry asked.

"Oh, not by a long shot," Mary said. "We'll discuss your punishment later, but for now... well, what you did was very brave. I'm proud of you, Harry."

"Thanks, Mom. I am sorry."

171

"You're a pretty remarkable kid, Harry Moon, and you have a destiny to fulfill," she said, ruffling his hair. Then, resuming her serious mood, she said: "Now, let me get your father and have you tell him the whole thing as well."

Harry nodded as she left the room. A wide smile came to his face. No matter what his punishment was, he would gladly take it.

In the end, any recompense his parents gave out was worth the hugs and love that came attached to it.

172

MARK ANDREW POE

The Adventures of Harry Moon author Mark Andrew Poe never thought about being a children's writer growing up. His dream was to love and care for animals, specifically his friends in the rabbit community.

Along the way, Mark became successful in all sorts of interesting careers. He entered the print and publishing world as a young man and his company did really, really well.

Mark became a popular and nationally sought-after health care advocate for the care and well-being of rabbits.

Years ago, Mark came up with the idea of a story about a young man with a special connection to a world of magic, all revealed through a remarkable rabbit friend. Mark worked on his idea for several years before building a collaborative creative team to help bring his idea to life. And Harry Moon was born.

In 2014, Mark began a multi-book print series project intended to launch *The Adventures of Harry Moon* into the youth marketplace as a hero defined by a love for a magic where love and 'DO NO EVIL' live. Today, Mark continues to work on the many stories of Harry Moon. He lives in suburban Chicago with his wife and his 25 rabbits.

BE SURE TO READ THE CONTINUING AND AMAZING ADVENTURES OF HARRY MOON

HARRY MOON  BOOK CLUB

Become a member of the
Harry Moon Book Club and receive another
of Harry's adventure every other month along
with a magician's hat full of goodies!

Hop over to www.harrymoon.com
and sign up today.

ALSO IN THE HARRY MOON LIBRARY:

Graphic novel